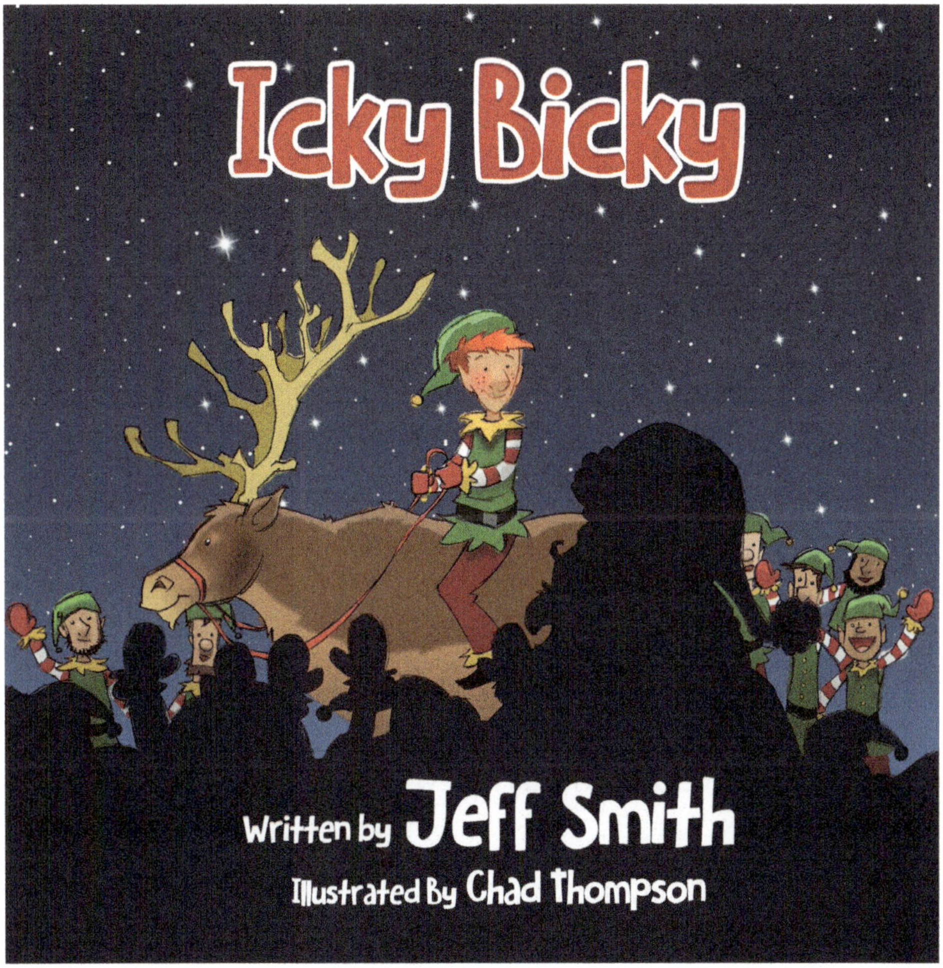
Icky Bicky
Written by Jeff Smith
Illustrated By Chad Thompson

Halo
Publishing International

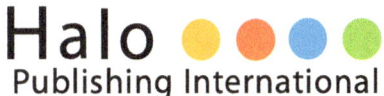

Copyright © 2015 Jeffrey B. Smith
Illustrated by Chad Thompson
All rights reserved.

The title of Work is registered as TXu1-335-199.

No part of this book may be reproduced in any manner without the written consent of the publisher except for brief excerpts in critical reviews or articles.

ISBN: 978-1-61244-424-6
Library of Congress Control Number: 2015916246

Printed in the United States of America

Published by Halo Publishing International
1100 NW Loop 410
Suite 700 - 176
San Antonio, Texas 78213
Toll Free 1-877-705-9647
Website: www.halopublishing.com
E-mail: contact@halopublishing.com

To Grandma Nette,
Thanks for all the wonderful Christmas Eves with Icky Bicky.
Luva, Luva!
Jeff

It was Christmas Eve and there Eloise sat,
rocking in a chair with her big yellow cat.

Now, most parents have it easy on Christmas Day.
The kids open presents and shout, "Hurray!"

Christmas at this poor house wasn't quite the same;
her kids had no presents, no toys and no games.

Eloise had lost the spirit of Christmas years ago.
She hadn't sent a letter to Santa because she didn't believe it was so.

She looked on her desk and sent from above
was a little white card in a little white glove.

She opened the card and what did she find?
Her children's Christmas list to Santa
with laughter and cheer in mind.

The list didn't mention a single toy.
No presents, just laughter and joy.

She thought to herself maybe this would be the way.
Send the letter to Santa and there would be a Christmas Day.

Now, Santa doesn't read the letters first;
they must be screened by the Elf Murphs.

The Elf Murphs are the smartest of the bunch.
They work so hard, they don't even take a lunch.

When they saw the letter from Eloise and her kids
it was a code 94716: a late Christmas card, heavens forbid.

Elf President Winky Scoot was consumed with the Christmas rush.
He was so surprised with the late letter, he began to blush.

You must realize elves never get mad
but when something bothers them, they blush real bad.

When the blushing was done,
Winky called in Bucky and Shock to have some final Christmas fun.

He told them, "This matter must be done without delay.
Santa is leaving soon because tomorrow is Christmas day."

Bucky and Shock left right away
but there remained a little elf waiting in Winky's office
with something to say.

"I don't understand why Santa has all the fun
while the elves make all the toys and are always on the run."

Winky had heard this a time or two before.
He told Icky Bicky, "Elves weren't born to ride in the sleigh and sore.

"We were born to make toys for Santa and that's all we will ever be,
so quit dreaming. Santa Clause you'll never be."

Icky Bicky left the office blushing from head to toe
when Winky ordered, "Get some rest or go outside and play in the snow."

As Icky Bicky walked outside, the blushing went away,
seeing Santa ride off with his reindeer and sleigh.

Bucky and Shock came running past,
but instead of being delivered to Santa,
the little white letter landed in Icky Bicky's lap.

As the elves all wondered what to do,
Icky Bicky went home, read the letter and started to snew.

Now snewing may not be known outside of Toyland
but when an elf snews, he can't feel his hands.

They say when snewing begins;
elves don't know when it will end.

So Icky Bicky sat in his house and started to wrap.
Soon he was tired and he took a nap.

He dreamt about wrapping presents but not for very long.
He woke up singing a Christmas song.

He walked outside and saw the elves were still sad.
They cried out, "Santa's going to be mad!"

Icky Bicky put all his presents in an elf sack,
snuck past the elves and into the sleigh shack.

He threw the presents in Santa's old sleigh
and grabbed the reserve reindeer that started to neigh.

Icky Bicky burst through the doors and the elves ran with fear;
wondering what he was doing with Santa's reserve reindeer.

With the reserve reindeer and the big elf sack,
he flew over Toyland and didn't look back.

When Icky Bicky arrived at the house,
he slipped down the chimney as quiet as a mouse.

He put the presents under the tree just like Santa does.
He even ate some cookies and grabbed a handful of fudge.

Unfortunately, Icky Bicky tripped and let out a shout.
And the little white letter fell out of his pocket pouch.

All the commotion woke up the kids.
Soon they came running in their little red bibs.

Icky Bicky quickly got out of sight
and watched with delight.

The presents were opened and fruit was inside
with liquorish for smiles and dots for eyes.

Eloise walked down stairs wondering what was going on.
She saw her kids laughing and burst into song.

Icky Bicky headed back to Toyland expecting cheers.
Instead, he found Santa waiting with all his reindeer.

Santa and the blushing elves started to shout,
"Icky Bicky what have you been doing flying about?"

Icky Bicky explained he saved Christmas day
for one poor family without delay.

"Icky Bicky for President of Toyland," a crowd of young elves chanted with glee.
He thought to himself, *Someday…maybe.*

Santa learned a few lessons that day.

First, you can count on an Elf to save the day.

However, the most important lesson learned of all
was fancy presents didn't mean a thing.
The joy of Christmas was what made the family sing.